Little Lola

By **Julie Saab**

Pictures By
David Gothard

Greenwillow Books
An Imprint of HarperCollins *Publishers*

Special thanks to Charissa Baker, Jos. A. Smith,
and our family for their enthusiasm and support.
And to Virginia and Paul for believing in us.

Little Lola
Text copyright © 2014 by Julie Saab
Illustrations copyright © 2014 by David Gothard
All rights reserved. Manufactured in China.
For information address HarperCollins Children's Books,
a division of HarperCollins Publishers,
10 East 53rd Street, New York, NY 10022.
www.harpercollinschildrens.com

Watercolors were used to prepare the full-color art.

The text type is 23-point Imperfect.

Library of Congress Cataloging-in-Publication Data is available.
ISBN 978-0-06-227457-1 (trade ed.)

14 15 16 17 18 SCP 10 9 8 7 6 5 4 3 2 1
First Edition

 Greenwillow Books

PING!

For Mabelle, Eloise, Dylan, and Anna,
and in loving memory of Esther Gothard

This is Little Lola. She woke up extra early today.

That was lucky, because she had big plans.

TO DO
- [x] stretch
- [x] read paper
- [x] hide
- [x] juggle
- [x] play games
- [ ] have an adventure

Lola! Where are you going?

Hooray! Lola is going to school!

There was a place
for everything and everyone
at school.

SQUEAK!

SHOW & TELL

Emily

Eloise

Mabelle

Anna

Aaron

Dylan

Paul

There was even a place
for a curious little cat.

Lola practiced writing,

reading,

adding,

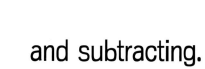

and subtracting.

YUM!

Lola practiced painting,

playing,

hiding,

swinging,

singing,

and sharing.

YUM!

Lola loved it all!

She loved story time

and show-and-tell
the best.

Lola had the
perfect surprise
to share with everyone.

SHOW & TELL

Aaron

Paul

Dylan

Anna

Mabelle

Emily

TA-DA!

Eloise

What a mess!
What a DISASTER!

But not for long.

Lola picked up,

and cleaned up,

and put everything back in its place.

(Well, almost.)

Good-bye, Little Lola!
See you tomorrow!